GONE FISHING

Earlene Long

Illustrated by Richard Brown

Houghton Mifflin Company Boston 1984

Library of Congress Cataloging in Publication Data

Long, Earlene, 1938–
  Gone fishing.

  Summary: A father and son go fishing with a big fish-
ing rod for daddy and a little one for the child.
  [1. Fathers and sons — Fiction. 2. Fishing — Fiction]
I. Brown, Richard Eric, 1946–   ill. II. Title.
PZ7.L8449Go   1984   [E]   83-22558
ISBN 0-395-35570-2

Printed in the United States of America

P 10 9 8 7 6 5 4 3 2 1

My big daddy.

Little me.

A big breakfast for my daddy.

A little breakfast for me.

A big fishing rod for my daddy.

A little fishing rod for me.

Leave a note for my mommy.

"Gone fishing," signed my daddy and me.

Worms in a can. Lunch in a box.

Fishing for my daddy and me.

Sun comes up on the water.

"It is shining on the lake. I see! I see!"

15

Worms on the hooks. Lines in the water.

Fishing for my daddy and me.

A big fish for my daddy.

A little fish for me.

Hooks and worms in the water.

Fishing for my daddy and me.

A big lunch for my daddy.

A little lunch for me.

Hooks and worms in the water.

Fishing for my daddy and me.

A little fish for my daddy.

A big fish for me.

Going home to my mommy.

We caught fish for her to see.

A big fish and a little fish for my daddy.

A little fish and a big fish for me.

Gone fishing, my daddy and me.